STORYTIME COLLECTION

STORYTIME COLLECTION

This book belongs to

_____

_____

Published in 2018
by Autumn Publishing
Cottage Farm
Sywell
NN6 0BJ
www.igloobooks.com

GUA009 0718
2 4 6 8 10 9 7 5 3
ISBN 978-1-78810-996-3

Printed and manufactured in China

Disney · PIXAR
INCREDIBLES 2

∞ STORYTIME COLLECTION ∞

It had been an exciting day for the Parr family, who were now on their way home. Unknown to them, something villainous was stirring under the surface of Municiberg…

… suddenly, from out of nowhere, the supervillain known as the Underminer burst through the ground in a giant machine called a tunneller. The family quickly changed into their supersuits and chased after him.

Violet, however, had to stay behind to look after baby Jack-Jack. "Oh, great," said the young Super, who would have liked to join in the action herself.

Meanwhile, the Underminer was causing havoc, burrowing beneath the city, breaking open bank vaults and taking all the money. "Consider yourselves Undermined!" cried the supervillain.

Mr. Incredible quickly appeared and punched his way into the tunneller. He grabbed the startled Underminer and threw him against the control panel, smashing it to pieces. The machine heaved forward and sped up!

With Mr. Incredible off-balance, the Underminer jumped into his escape pod and got away. Mr. Incredible inspected the ruined controls and saw the tunneller was headed up to the surface. There was no way to stop it!

The tunneller smashed through the ground and hit the monorail, knocking a train off the tracks. In a flash, Frozone appeared and created an ice bridge to get the passengers to safety. The tunneller, however, kept on going.

"It's headed for City Hall!" cried Mr. Incredible, who had been joined inside the tunneller by the rest of his family. With Elastigirl's help, Mr. Incredible pulled the boiler loose from the engine causing a massive explosion!

Luckily, Violet wrapped them all in a
force field to protect them. The plan
worked, as the tunneller stopped
inches from City Hall.

As the Incredibles left the broken
machine, they were quickly
surrounded by the police.

The Supers were blamed for wrecking the city and for not capturing the Underminer. "You would have preferred we do nothing?" asked Mr. Incredible.

"Without a doubt," a government official replied.

Unhappy at their treatment, the Parr family went back to the motel they'd been living in since their house was destroyed. Agent Dicker, who'd followed them back from City Hall, revealed that the National Supers Agency was being shut down. In two weeks, the family would be on their own.

At dinner, the family were talking about their future. "We wanna fight bad guys," said Dash, enthusiastically.

"Super Heroes are illegal," replied Helen. "Whether it's fair or not, that's the law."

After they'd eaten and the children had gone to bed, Bob and Helen spoke about finding a new house and getting jobs. Just then, Lucius, also known as Frozone, appeared. He had news about a business tycoon who wanted to make Supers legal. "He wants to meet tonight," said Lucius.

Mr. Incredible, Elastigirl and Frozone arrived at a massive building belonging to DevTech. The owner, Winston Deavor, loved Supers and wanted to make them legal again because his parents died as a result of a robbery. "If Super Heroes had not been forced underground, it never would have happened," he said. "I'm sure of it."

Winston's plan involved getting the public to see the Supers in action. Evelyn, his tech-genius sister, showed them all a small camera for their supersuits that would record their heroic acts. Winston then announced that the first mission would go to Elastigirl.

Having arrived back at the motel, Bob was trying to persuade Helen to accept the job. "A few hours ago, you were saying it was over and being a Super Hero was a fantasy!" he cried. "Now you get the offer of a lifetime and you don't know?"

"You know it's crazy, right?" replied Helen. "To help my family, I've got to leave it; to fix the law, I've got to break it."

Bob reassured her by saying he would take care of the kids while she was away. Relieved to have her husband's support, Helen called Winston to accept the job.

The next day, Winston sent a limo to pick up the family and take them to their new home. When they arrived, they saw it had an indoor pool, as well as multiple hidden exits. "Isn't this a bit much?" asked Helen.

"The important thing is we're out of the motel," replied Bob.

Leaving her family to settle into their new home, Helen found her new supersuit and a jet-powered, all-electric Elasticycle! She was soon ready to leave, but not before saying goodbye to Bob. "You'll be great," said her husband.

"I will be great," smiled Elastigirl. "And you will, too."

Elastigirl zoomed away to the airport, where Winston and Evelyn were waiting for her. Winston explained her first mission would be in the city of New Urbem. "You wanna make a big crime-fighting statement, you go where the crime is big," he added.

The next morning at breakfast, Bob told Dash and Violet that their mum had left for a new job. "She's an advocate for Super Heroes," he explained.

This didn't make sense to Violet, as she knew Supers were illegal. "So, Mum is going out, illegally, to explain why she shouldn't be illegal?"

Bob wasn't sure how best to answer, but luckily for him, the school bus arrived. Violet and Dash rushed out the door.

Meanwhile, in New Urbem, Elastigirl was desperately trying to stop a runaway hovertrain! Riding her Elasticycle, she sped through tunnels, across roofs and even over a crane.

After finally catching up with the speeding train, Elastigirl stretched herself into a parachute to slow it down. The hovertrain screeched to a halt just seconds from disaster!

As Elastigirl checked to make sure the passengers were all okay, she noticed a message appear on a control panel:

Welcome back, Elastigirl — The Screenslaver.

Back home, Bob was helping Dash with his maths homework, but the sums had confused him. "It's okay, Dad," said Dash. "I'll wait for Mum to get back."

Bob then went to read Jack-Jack a bedtime story. But before Bob had barely begun, the baby had dozed off.

Feeling exhausted and missing Helen, Bob fell asleep on the sofa. Not long after, Jack-Jack snuck out of his cot and went outside. He'd spotted a raccoon rooting through the bins. With its black-mask face, it looked just like a burglar and Jack-Jack was determined to catch it. What was more remarkable was that Jack-Jack had walked straight through the glass!

Moments later, a loud CRASH from outside woke Bob. He jumped up and rushed outside to find Jack-Jack firing laser beams from his eyes towards the startled raccoon! "You have powers!" shouted Bob, happily. "Yeah, baby!"

His excitement was short-lived as he realised that if Jack-Jack was developing super powers, he had a huge problem on his hands.

No sooner had Bob taken Jack-Jack back inside, Helen rang
to make sure everything was under control. "Amazing as it may seem, it
has been quite uneventful," lied Bob. "How about you?"

"I saved a runaway train!" cried Helen, unable to contain her excitement.
"It was SO GREAT!" After recounting the story, she said
to Bob, "I couldn't have done this if you hadn't taken over so well."

With Helen believing Bob was doing such a good job, he was determined
to succeed. So, he stayed up all night figuring out how to help Dash with
his homework. The next day, Bob sat down with his son once more.
By the time Dash left for school, he had finished all his homework.
Bob was proud of his son and proud of himself, too!

Back in New Urbem, Elastigirl was being interviewed about her daring train rescue. Suddenly, a hypnotic pattern appeared on every screen in the studio. The interviewer, Chad Brentley, spoke in a robotic voice. "We are controlled by screens. And screens are controlled by me, the Screenslaver."

Elastigirl was about to slap Chad out of his hypnotised state, when the Screenslaver threatened to crash an ambassador's helicopter. Elastigirl rushed from the studio to the roof.

Upon reaching the roof, Elastigirl saw the ambassador's helicopter and leapt inside. The pilot was hypnotised by the screens until Elastigirl smashed them. She then grabbed the ambassador, swung out of the spinning craft and landed safely. Yet again, she'd saved everyone!

After another stunning success, Winston introduced Elastigirl to a group of Supers. He also believed now was the time to push to make Supers legal. "We're going to have a summit at sea!" he cried. "We'll gather leaders and Supers from all over the world."

Elastigirl was happy things were going so well, but knew the Screenslaver was still out there. She had a plan to deal with this, though. Taking Evelyn to one side, Elastigirl said she could capture the villain by tracking his broadcast signal. All she needed was a device that could do it. "I can get your contraption together," replied Evelyn.

That night, with Evelyn's tracker in hand, Elastigirl set her trap for the Screenslaver. She called in for a remote interview with Chad Brentley from the roof of his studio. But, as before, the Screenslaver took control of the broadcast. The tracker lit up and showed the signal's origin. Elastigirl set off and arrived at the apartment that was the source of the signal. "Find anything interesting?" It was the Screenslaver.

The pair began to fight, but the
Screenslaver slipped away. Elastigirl
chased after him and, seconds later, the apartment blew up!
All the evidence had been destroyed. In the confusion, Elastigirl
was able to capture and finally unmask the villain. Behind the
mask was a very baffled young man. He insisted he was innocent,
even as the police arrested him.

Back home, Bob learned something that shocked him. His former super car, the Incredibile, was in the hands of a car collector. "They told me it was destroyed!" he cried, before rummaging in a box and finding the car's remote control.

Dash snatched it from him. "Which button launches the rockets?" he asked, excitedly.

Suddenly, Violet screamed. Jack-Jack had transformed into a monster and was chasing her down the stairs! She and Dash quickly realised Bob had been hiding the baby's new powers from them. They both told Bob he needed some help. Not knowing who else to turn to, Bob spoke to his friend, Lucius, who suggested Edna might know what to do.

So, Bob took Jack-Jack to see Edna Mode, where he asked if she could babysit. Edna was appalled. "I'm not a baby person, Robert!" she cried. However, upon seeing Jack-Jack morph to look just like her, Edna's heart melted and she changed her mind. "Auntie Edna will take care of everything," she cooed to Jack-Jack.

Meanwhile, Winston and Evelyn were throwing a massive party to celebrate the capture of the Screenslaver. But Elastigirl and Evelyn were busy watching footage of the villain's lair from her suit cameras and something felt wrong. "Look," said Elastigirl. "One of the Screenslaver's monitors was tuned into my suit cam. Isn't the suit cam closed circuit?"

"Maybe he hacked it?" shrugged Evelyn.

Something still didn't feel right to Elastigirl. "All the Screenslaver needs to hypnotise someone is a screen." She picked up Screenslaver's goggles and examined them. Small screens had been built into the lenses!

Without warning, Evelyn forced the goggles on Elastigirl. Bright lights flashed and Elastigirl was suddenly hypnotised.

In the morning, after a night's uninterrupted sleep, Bob returned to Edna's house to find that she had enjoyed babysitting Jack-Jack. She'd even created a supersuit that could anticipate his powers and send alerts.

Edna put Jack-Jack in the testing chamber and handed Bob a tracker. The tablet lit up: *Replication Event.*

A moment later, little Jack-Jack multiplied into lots of Jack-Jacks!

Elastigirl awoke in a freezing room. She couldn't stretch to escape. If she tried, she'd break! Evelyn was glaring at her through a glass wall. "So you're the Screenslaver," said Elastigirl, who asked why Evelyn had betrayed Winston and the Super Heroes.

"Super Heroes keep us weak," she replied, and then went on to explain how she used a pizza delivery guy to play the Screenslaver.

"Are you going to kill me?" asked Elastigirl.

Evelyn smiled, evilly. "Nah, using you is better. You're going to help make Supers illegal forever." She then placed Elastigirl back under hypnosis.

Bob had brought Jack-Jack home, and was showing Violet and Dash how to use Edna's tracker. As the kids were playing with the device, the phone rang. It was Evelyn. "Elastigirl's in trouble," she said. "Meet me on the ship."

"The ship at DevTech," replied Bob. "I'll be there in fifteen minutes!"
He called Lucius to watch the kids, before rushing away.

Soon after, six hypnotised Supers, all under Evelyn's control, arrived to kidnap the kids. Frozone arrived just in time and created a giant wall of ice to block their path. It wasn't long before they'd broken through, but luckily, it was enough time for the Incredibile to burst through the living room! Dash had summoned it with the remote control. The kids were able to escape, but Frozone was captured and a pair of hypno-goggles were slapped over his eyes.

Having no idea what was happening back at the house, Mr. Incredible
met Evelyn at the DevTech yacht, eager to find his wife.

As Evelyn led him to the ballroom, Elastigirl suddenly appeared and
pounced on her husband. He tried to dodge her attacks, but she was
too fast. "Helen!" he cried, confused. "It's me!"

Elastigirl ignored him and slid a pair of hypno-goggles over
Mr. Incredible's eyes. He fell silent and still.

The kids knew their parents were in trouble, so they used the Incredibile to get to the DevTech yacht as quickly as possible. By the time they arrived, the ship had already left. But, the Incredibile wasn't just any old car. "Follow that boat," said Dash to the vehicle. The car suddenly sped off the pier, landed with a SPLASH in the water and sailed towards the ship.

On board, Winston was welcoming all the delegates. Soon, it was time for the ceremony to begin. "I thank all of you for representing your nation's commitment to Super Heroes," he said.

Moments later, the kids boarded the boat and began the search for their parents. But Jack-Jack wandered off and Dash had to chase after him. Suddenly, Violet was attacked by a hypnotised Super called Voyd.

Voyd opened a series of holes in space to trap the young Super. But Violet fought back, blocking each of the voids with a force field! Dash quickly returned to help and the pair of them worked together and defeated Voyd. With the Super beaten, the pair rushed off to find baby Jack-Jack.

In the conference room, the International Super Hero Accord had just been signed. "The world is Super again!" declared Winston. But as the crowd gathered for a photo, Evelyn put a hypnotic pattern on the screens, entrancing everyone.

The world watched as Elastigirl, Mr. Incredible and Frozone, all still under Evelyn's control, delivered a dire message. "We no longer serve you," said Frozone. "We serve only us!"

With everyone starting to panic, Evelyn ordered the Supers to speed up the yacht and destroy the controls. The ship was on course to crash into the city!

Suddenly, the kids ran in and saw their parents standing over the smashed controls. Jack-Jack floated over to his mum and removed her goggles. No longer hypnotised, Elastigirl snatched the masks off Mr. Incredible and Frozone. They, too, were soon back to normal.

Elastigirl quickly changed into her red supersuit – the Incredibles were reunited and would fight together!

Evelyn watched on from her control room. Angry her plan might be foiled, she ordered the remaining hypnotised Supers to attack the Incredibles. By working as a family, the Incredibles were able to remove the hypno-goggles from the other Supers, one-by-one, until all of them were no longer under Evelyn's control.

Now the Supers were all
free and the ship was about to crash, Evelyn escaped the
boat in a jet that was hidden on the ship. With Voyd's help, Elastigirl
was able to enter the cockpit and confront Evelyn. "The reputations of
the Supers are ruined," taunted Evelyn. "You will never become legal."
She then kicked Elastigirl, knocking her over.

On the yacht, the Supers were trying to stop the ship from crashing into
the city. An idea suddenly came to Mr. Incredible, who jumped into the
water and used all his strength to move the rudder. The ship began to turn.

In the jet, Elastigirl was struggling to breathe as the plane went higher and higher. So, thinking quickly, she grabbed a flare gun and fired it at Evelyn's oxygen tank. The tank ruptured and threw the villain through the cockpit's windshield.

Elastigirl quickly launched herself out of the plane and caught Evelyn in mid-air. Just as the pair were about to hit the water, Voyd caught them both in a portal, sending them tumbling safely onto the deck of the ship.

With all the Supers now working together, the ship turned
even further and, with the help of a giant snowbank created
by Frozone, it came to a grinding halt just in front of the city.
Everyone was safe and the police came along and arrested
the real Screenslaver.

The public now saw that Supers were a good thing and they quickly became heroes to everybody once more. A judge also thanked them for their extraordinary service and restored their legal status!

STOCKS

MUNICIBE

EVENING EDITION   TUESDAY, SEPTEMBER 2ND

SUPERS

The Incredibles were now ready
to take on anything that came
their way and they would do
so together, as a family.

COLLECT THEM ALL!

With 7 more exciting titles to choose from, you'll want to complete your Storytime Collection!

Will Simba ever become king?

Will Rapunzel learn who she truly is?

Will Moana be able to save the ocean?

Can Anna and Elsa stop an eternal winter?

Will Mowgli defeat Shere Khan?

How far will a father go for his son?

Will Belle be able to break the curse?

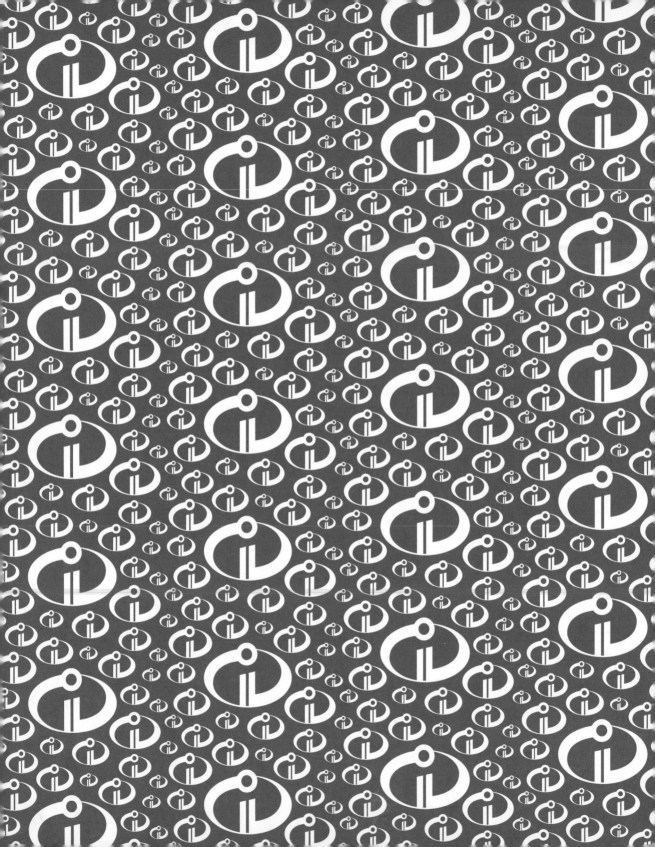